WELCOME TO
PASSPORT TO READING
A beginning reader's ticket to a brand-new world!

Every book in this program is designed to build read-along and read-alone skills, level by level, through engaging and enriching stories. As the reader turns each page, he or she will become more confident with new vocabulary, sight words, and comprehension.

These PASSPORT TO READING levels will help you choose the perfect book for every reader.

READING TOGETHER
Read short words in simple sentence structures together to begin a reader's journey.

READING OUT LOUD
Encourage developing readers to sound out words in more complex stories with simple vocabulary.

READING INDEPENDENTLY
Newly independent readers gain confidence reading more complex sentences with higher word counts.

READY TO READ MORE
Readers prepare for chapter books with fewer illustrations and longer paragraphs.

This book features sight words from the educator-supported Dolch Sight Words List. This encourages the reader to recognize commonly used vocabulary words, increasing reading speed and fluency.

For more information, please visit passporttoreadingbooks.com.

Enjoy the journey!

Little, Brown and Company

Hachette Book Group
1290 Avenue of the Americas, New York, NY 10104
Visit us at lb-kids.com

Little, Brown and Company is a division of Hachette Book Group, Inc.
The Little, Brown name and logo are trademarks of Hachette Book Group, Inc.

The publisher is not responsible for websites (or their content)
that are not owned by the publisher.

First Edition: September 2015

Library of Congress Cataloging-in-Publication Data

Sazaklis, John.
  Meet High Tide / by John Sazaklis & Steve Foxe. — First edition.
    pages cm. — (Passport to reading. Level 1)
  "Transformers Rescue Bots."
  Summary: "Optimus Prime wants his friend High Tide to teach the Rescue Bots about water rescues. But first, High Tide must learn about teamwork in order to help protect the people of Griffin Rock"—Provided by publisher.
  ISBN 978-0-316-41090-8 (trade pbk.) — ISBN 978-0-316-38829-0 (ebook) — ISBN 978-0-316-38830-6 (library edition ebook)
  I. Foxe, Steve. II. Transformers, Rescue Bots (Television program) III. Title.
PZ7.S27587Me 2015
[E]—dc23

                                                2015011642

10 9 8 7 6 5 4 3 2

CW

Printed in the United States of America

Passport to Reading titles are leveled by independent reviewers
applying the standards developed by Irene Fountas and Gay Su Pinnell in *Matching
Books to Readers: Using Leveled Books in Guided Reading*, Heinemann, 1999.

Licensed By:

TRANSFORMERS
RESCUE BOTS

Meet High Tide

Adapted by **John Sazaklis**
& Steve Foxe

Based on the episode
"Turning the Tide" written by
Steve Granat & Cydne Clark

L B

LITTLE, BROWN AND COMPANY
New York Boston

Attention, Rescue Bots fans!
Look for these words when you read this book.
Can you spot them all?

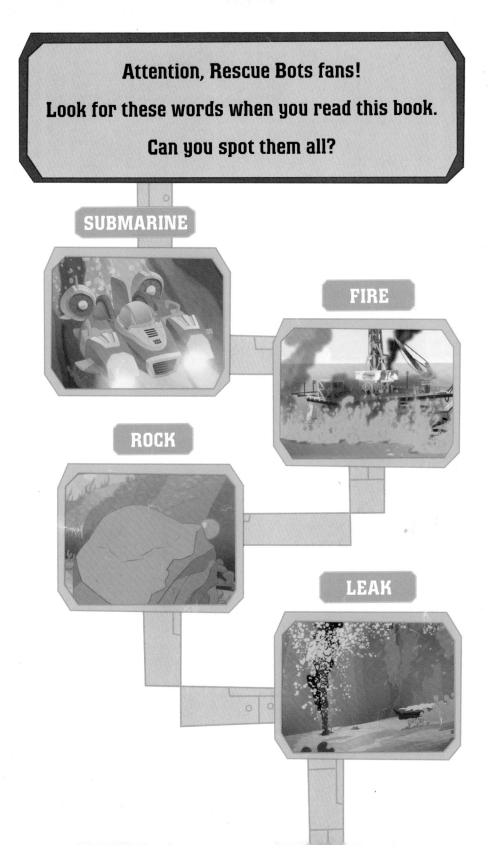

SUBMARINE

FIRE

ROCK

LEAK

The Rescue Bots are
a special group of Autobots.
Optimus Prime gave them a mission
to serve and protect humans.

The Rescue Bots are named
Heatwave, Chase, Boulder,
and Blades.

A new Autobot has arrived!

His name is High Tide.

He turns into a submarine called
Sea Lab that dives underwater.

High Tide can also steer a big ship.

The ship turns into a huge Mega-Bot!

One day, Doc Greene asks
the Rescue Bots for help.
He thinks an old oil rig
might fall apart.

Heatwave takes his friends
across the water.

They get stuck in a whirlpool!

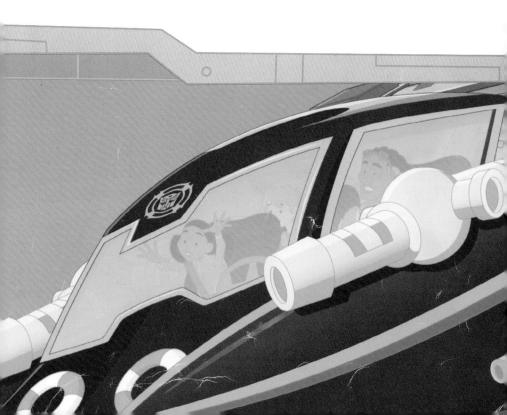

High Tide rushes to the rescue!

He scoops Heatwave out of the water.

Heatwave will not stop
moving in High Tide's hands.
High Tide drops him in the water
with a splash!

Heatwave is puzzled.

"Who are you?" Heatwave asks.

"My name is High Tide.

I am here to train you."

"Says who?" asks Heatwave.

"I do," says Optimus Prime.

"High Tide can help you learn

about water rescues."

Heatwave does not think
his team needs training.

High Tide will prove him wrong!
He will whip these Bots
into tip-top shape!

"Ten-hut!" High Tide shouts.

He yells so loud that Blades gets scared.

Blades crashes into an oil drum.

"Servo, oil spill!" High Tide yells.

His helper Bot, Servo, cleans up the mess.

Servo looks just like a robot dog!

High Tide teaches Boulder
how to use a surfboard.
Boulder messes up!

High Tide stops Boulder from falling
into a deep trench!

"What kind of Rescue Bots
need to be rescued?" High Tide asks.

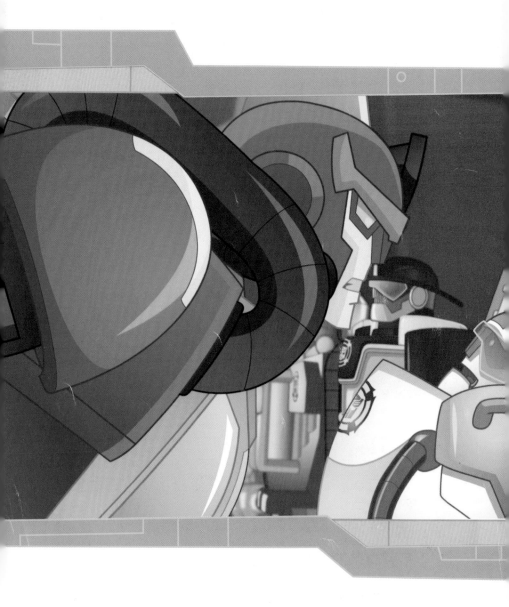

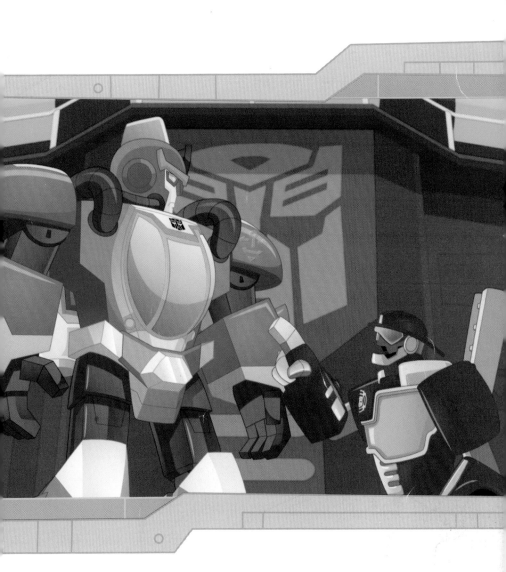

Heatwave is mad.

"You are a bully," Heatwave says.

"I do not want to train
with you anymore."

He storms off.

High Tide faces the rest of the crew.

"Does anyone else want to quit?"

he asks.

The other Bots stay put.

The emergency phone rings!

There is a fire at the oil rig.

Doc Greene and Frankie are trapped,

and oil is leaking into the ocean!

"I will fix this alone," High Tide says.

He dives down toward the leaking pipe.

High Tide tries to cover
the hole with a rock.
It does not stop the leak.
He needs help.

Heatwave arrives at the oil rig.

Heatwave blasts through the flames!

Then he rescues Doc Greene and Frankie.

Heatwave cares about humans.

That is what makes him a great Rescue Bot.

Now that the fire is out,

the leak needs to be fixed.

The Rescue Bots try to fix the leak.

They alone are not strong enough!

They need High Tide's help!

Together, they plug the leak.

"I am sorry.

I was a bully," High Tide says.

"Teamwork gets the job done!"

Optimus Prime asks High Tide

to stay in Griffin Rock

and learn more about teamwork.

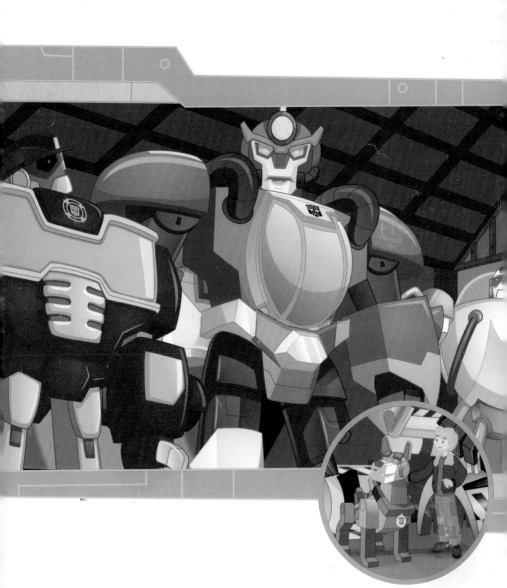

Heatwave forgives High Tide.

"Welcome to the team," Heatwave says.

"We have much more to learn from you, too."

Servo also looks happy to stay in Griffin Rock!